Joseph and Koza

First published in this edition 1984
Published by Hamish Hamilton Children's Books
Garden House 57–59 Long Acre London WC2E 9JZ
Text copyright © 1969, 1970 by Isaac Bashevis Singer
Illustrations copyright © 1984 by Donna Diamond
All Rights Reserved

British Library Cataloguing in Publication Data
Singer, Isaac Bashevis
Joseph and Koza
I. Title
813'.54[J]   PS3569.I5437
ISBN 0-241-11050-5

Typeset by Katerprint Co Ltd, Oxford
Printed in Great Britain by
BAS Printers Ltd,
Over Wallop, Stockbridge, Hampshire

Isaac Bashevis Singer

Joseph and Koza

Translated from the Yiddish by
the author and Elizabeth Shub

Illustrated by Donna Diamond

Hamish Hamilton · London

Joseph and Koza

It happened long, long ago in the land which is now Poland. The country was covered with thick forests and swamps and the people were divided into many tribes that waged bloody battles among themselves. They fought with bows and arrows, swords and spears because in those days they had neither rifles nor guns.

The roads were dangerous. Highwaymen lay in wait for merchants to rob and murder them. Often, travellers were attacked by wolves, bears, boars, and other wild beasts. And there were the many warlocks and witches who had sworn allegiance to Baba Yaga the Terrible and other Evil Powers. No one in all of Poland could read or write. The people worshipped idols of stone, clay, and wood, to whom they sacrificed not only animals but human beings as well.

The most powerful tribe in Poland inhabited Mazovia, a huge tract of land near the river Vistula. Mazovia was ruled by a Chieftain called Wilk, who had a wife named Wilkova. Wilk was a tall man with a ruddy face and flaxen hair. He wore a moustache whose tips reached down to his shoulders. Other chieftains in the land possessed crowns made of gold, silver, and precious stones, but Wilk's crown was a hollow gourd with notches cut in its rim to hold beeswax candles. The candles were lit when Wilk wore the crown.

Wilk kept a witch and stargazer called Zla, and the Chieftain never made a move without consulting her. It was said that Zla could perform miracles. She rode in a carriage drawn by wolves and used a living snake as a whip.

Once each year it was the custom of the Mazovians to sacrifice their most beautiful maiden to the

Joseph and Koza

Joseph and Koza

river Vistula. The people gathered at the river's shore. They drank wine, beer, mead, killed and roasted pigs, sang and danced all day long. Late in the day, when the sun was about to sink below the horizon, they brought forth the maiden. She was carried to a high cliff overlooking the river and was thrown in. The Mazovians believed that this sacrifice would pacify the evil spirits of the Vistula.

It was the witch Zla who each year chose the most beautiful maiden of the land. First she read the stars for signs and then she consulted with the devil. No one ever questioned Zla's choice.

Wilk had seven sons, but only one daughter, Koza. Koza had golden hair and blue eyes, and the Chieftain and his wife loved her above all else. When Koza was seventeen, and the time had come for her to marry, many kings' sons came to Mazovia to woo her. They competed in feats of prowess to see who would win her hand. One young suitor tore a wolf in half with his bare hands. Another strangled an ox. A third tore up a tree by the roots. Finally the young men fought each other with swords. They were as cruel to one another as they had been to the animals.

Koza was forced to witness these wild tournaments, but none of the young princes pleased her. She was kind-hearted by nature and hated bloodshed.

Every year on the first night of the month of Kwiecien (our April, more or less), the witch Zla studied the stars to determine who was the prettiest girl in Mazovia. That spring as she searched the heavens on the appointed night, she suddenly moaned out loud. It was Koza that the stars had revealed to her.

When Wilk heard that he must sacrifice his daughter, he was grief-stricken. His wife fainted away. But Koza tried to comfort her parents. She said to her father: "If by giving my life to the Vistula, I can satisfy the evil spirits and serve our people, I will gladly do so."

The sacrificial ceremony always took place at the

Joseph and Koza

Joseph and Koza

beginning of summer, on the first day of the month of Lipiec, or July. During the ninety days of waiting, the chosen maiden lived in a large tent erected in an apple orchard not far from the river bank. The highborn young ladies of Mazovia came to keep Koza company. They sang and danced for her, wove wreaths of flowers, and brought her gifts to sweeten the long vigil.

One day a wanderer appeared at the gate of Wilk's palace. He was tall, had a black beard, long black hair, and black eyes. He carried a pouch on his back, and a large scroll under his arm. The Mazovians had never before seen a scroll and they looked at it in amazement. The stranger told the guards that he had come to see Chieftain Wilk.

"Who are you? Where do you come from?" he was asked.

"From Jerusalem."

The guards informed Wilk, who sent for the stranger.

"What is your name?" Wilk asked.

"Joseph."

"Joseph? I've never heard of such a name. Who are you? And what do you want?"

Joseph replied, "I'm a Jew and I come from the city of Jerusalem. I am a goldsmith by profession. I make bracelets, brooches, and rings. I am on my way from Krakow, where I made a crown with golden horns for the King. I spent over a year in his palace, and there I learned to speak your language."

"What are you carrying under your arm?" Wilk asked.

"A scroll."

"What is a scroll?"

"This one bears God's commandments."

"Which God's commandments? Is he made of bone? Wood? Stone? Copper?"

"My God cannot be made by human hands," Joseph replied. "He has always lived. He is the creator of the earth, the sky, the sea, of all living things, men and animals. Many, many ages ago He revealed himself to Moses on Mount Sinai and gave him His commandments."

Joseph and Koza

Joseph and Koza

Wilk did not know what to make of all this. Finally he said to Joseph: "I would order a crown like the one you made for the King of Krakow, but this year is a time of mourning for me. Return next year and I will have you make a crown for me."

"Why are you in mourning?" Joseph asked.

"In sixty days my daughter Koza is to be sacrificed to the Vistula."

"The God of Israel has forbidden human sacrifice!" Joseph protested.

"How can that be?" Wilk asked. "If we fail to present the river with our most beautiful maiden, the Evil Powers will see that we get neither rain nor sunshine, and so our fields will give no harvest. If we do not bring this sacrifice to the Vistula, the river will overflow. It will be cold in the summertime and our crops will perish."

"Nonsense!" Joseph exclaimed. "It is God who makes the crops grow. God does not demand that a young maiden be drowned. It is a sin!"

Wilk pondered Joseph's words, and then he said:

"It is true that I am the ruler of my people, but I know little about such matters. The wisest person in my country is the witch Zla. I will order my servants to provide you with food and a tent to sleep in, and tomorrow you will speak to Zla. But remember, she reads the stars and serves Baba Yaga and other powers of evil. Should you anger her, she can destroy you or turn you into a hedgehog, a rat, or a frog. We all fear her, because the devil and the abyss are the sources of her strength."

"I do not fear her," Joseph replied. "The word of God is stronger than all witches and devils."

When Wilk's headmen and councillors learned about Joseph and what he had said, there was fear and confusion among them. Some insisted that the stranger was a messenger of doom and should be executed at once. Others thought that his words should be put to the test. After long arguing, it was decided that a debate should be held between Joseph and Zla in the presence of the entire court, presided over by Chieftain Wilk himself. Joseph immediately consented. At first Zla insisted that it was beneath her dignity to debate with an unknown intruder. But Wilk ordered her to appear.

The debate was fierce and lasted from morning till night. Zla denied the existence of one god and pointed out how vengeful the spirits of the Vistula were, particularly Topiel, whose palace was at the bottom of the river. She claimed that the maidens sacrificed to the Vistula did not really die but became the wives and concubines of Topiel. They danced, sang, and played music to keep him entertained. As proof of Topiel's power, she related how, at the winter and summer solstices, Baba Yaga herself visited the King of the river. She came flying to the Vistula in a huge mortar, holding a pestle the size of a pine tree in one hand and, in the other, a giant broom with which she swept away the light of the world. Who could dare rebel against such power?

Joseph and Koza

Joseph and Koza

Zla warned that unless Koza was given to the river on the first day of the month of Lipiec, there would be a storm, floods, thunder and lightning such as never before. Hailstones as large as rocks would destroy the crops. And should any grain survive the storm, it would be consumed by locusts, worms and field mice.

Joseph unrolled the scroll he had brought with him. He explained what it said in the language of the land. "God created the world in six days. God does not demand human sacrifices. He instructs man not to kill, steal, or bear false witness, but to honour his father and mother, and to be just and help those in need." Turning to Zla, he said: "No matter how strong the devils are, it is God who rules the world, not they. And the maidens you throw into the Vistula—they drown and rot. No devil can keep them alive under the water. The Vistula is not deep. Look carefully and you will see their bones."

The sun was moving toward the West, but the

Joseph and Koza

debate continued. Wilk's followers were divided into two camps. The older ones sided with Zla; the younger ones were with Joseph. When Joseph saw that his arguments could not convince them all, he said: "My lords, I can prove to you that the truth is on my side."

"How can you prove it?" asked Chieftain Wilk.

"The grain is harvested in the month of Sierpien. Wait until the end of Sierpien before you sacrifice the maiden. If the plagues Zla has prophesied occur, you will throw Koza into the Vistula and I myself will accept death at your hands because I misled you. But should these catastrophes not take place, you will have proof that I am right and that the words I read to you are the words of the true God."

Upon hearing this, Zla flew into a rage and began threatening Mazovia with even greater misfortunes. But Wilk lifted his sceptre, which was made of amber, and announced: "It will be as Joseph has said. The sacrifice of Koza is postponed until the end of Sierpien. Until that time, Joseph is to be imprisoned in the dungeon."

It was the law that once the Chieftain lifted his sceptre and spoke, nothing further must be said. All were silent. Only Zla could not contain her anger, and she screamed: "By the end of the month of Sierpien, Mazovia will be a desert!"

The Princess Koza and her ladies-in-waiting had not been present at the debate, but they soon learned what had taken place. Koza was prepared to give her life, but nevertheless, deep in her heart, she was afraid. She wanted neither to die nor to become one of Topiel's many wives and live in his underwater palace. When Joseph's words were repeated to her, she was filled with gratitude and love for him. She prayed to the gods of Mazovia that what he had said be true. Her ladies prayed with her.

Meanwhile, the days were mild and sunny. The sky was blue. It rained several times, but there was no flood. Each time clouds gathered, Zla insisted

Joseph and Koza

Joseph and Koza

that the storm was beginning, but the rain always stopped and the sky became clear again.

The month of Sierpien, our August, approached and the grain fields of Mazovia grew dense, golden, and ripe. The peasants had already begun to harvest the fields. They followed their usual rituals to ensure a good crop. Each village had its wooden rooster, decorated with green stalks of wheat and rye and tender twigs from fruit trees. The peasant girls, dancing around the rooster, sprayed water on it through a sieve. The Mazovians believed that in addition to Baba Yaga there were many lesser *babas*, as well as little imps called *dziads*, who lived in the furrows of the fields and who could do terrible damage unless they were exorcised through incantations and special ceremonies.

Although the time Joseph had set was almost at an end, Zla did not give up. She continued to prophesy that before Sierpien was out, the Vistula would overflow. She warned that day would become dark as night and that from the forest would come *babuks* riding vipers. They would destroy the sheaves of grain, the peasants' huts, the haystacks, and the granaries. Topiel himself, his face red, his beard white, with the wings of an eagle and the feet of a bear, would emerge from the Vistula. He would strangle children and kill the cattle. The river would spread itself over all the land.

On the twentieth day of Sierpien, Koza asked to be taken to her father. She begged him for permission to visit Joseph in his dungeon. Wilk agreed and sent two of her ladies with her. When Koza was shown into Joseph's cell, she found him sitting and writing on parchment with a quill. Koza had never seen a quill, ink, parchment. She fell on her knees before him, and both ladies knelt beside her. "Joseph," she said, "you are the greatest god of all." She began to weep and kiss his sandals.

Joseph made her rise. "I am not a god. There are no gods. One God creates us all," he said.

"Do you have a wife?" Koza asked.

"No, Koza, I am not married."

"Then I wish to be your wife."

Joseph and Koza

Joseph and Koza

"As it is destined, so will it be," Joseph replied.

He took three golden bracelets from his pack. One of them was set with a jewelled Star of David. He placed it on Koza's wrist and presented each of her companions with one of the remaining bracelets.

Since Joseph was convinced that Koza would not be drowned, that there would be no reason for Wilk to be in mourning, he had spent his time in prison making a golden crown for Mazovia's ruler. The Mazovians had no alphabet of their own, so Joseph had engraved the crown with Wilk's name in Hebrew letters, as well as the figure of a wolf, because Wilk meant wolf.

Excitement grew in Mazovia as the end of Sierpien approached. Those who no longer believed in Zla—mostly the young—sang, danced, and were confident of Joseph's final victory. The harvest, an especially plentiful one, had been gathered by now. The women began to grind the grain into flour. As always after harvest time, the evenings were devoted to games and festivity. Riddles were asked, stories were told. It was the custom that the girl who had harvested the last furrow became a *baba*. She blackened her face with soot, braided thistles into her hair, and carried a large witch's hoop. One of the boys impersonated a rooster. He attached wings to his shoulders, put a comb on his head, and tied spurs to his heels. He crowed and flapped, and made believe he was about to attack the girl *baba*, while she cackled like a hen and plucked feathers from his fake wings. Later the harvesters and threshers built a huge bonfire on which they roasted sides of pork and chestnuts. They drank mead and beer. The nights were as dark as the days were bright, and falling stars were frequently seen. The frogs croaked with human voices. Despite Zla's prophecy that any day the evil spirits of the Vistula would emerge to bring havoc, the young people went bathing in the river at night.

The older people who still believed in Zla

Joseph and Koza

warned that Sierpien was not yet over. They were certain the catastrophe would come. Many of them left their valley homes and camped on the hilltops to save themselves from the deluge. Others pointed out that it was not yet too late to choose another fair maiden to throw to the Vistula.

Zla continued to shower her curses on Joseph. She foretold that on the last day of Sierpien the sun would be extinguished, the moon would fall out of the sky, the trees would wither, and everything alive would perish. The waters of the Vistula would turn yellow and hot as boiling sulphur, and cover the entire earth.

The last day of Sierpien was the most beautiful of all. Not a single cloud marred the blue sky. The birds sang endlessly. The air was sweet as honey. Yet, until night fell, Zla was sure the flood would come. When the golden sun set behind the Vistula, she tore her hair, wailed, screamed, and whirled about in frenzy, but the world did not come to an end. Throughout Mazovia the news spread of

Joseph's victory and of his coming marriage to Koza. Zla was so humiliated that she hid in a deep cave.

Now that Joseph had been proven right, his freedom was restored and Wilk was prepared to give him his daughter in marriage. But there were many obstacles. Some of the older courtiers and their wives remained on the side of Zla, and the witch sent word from her cave that Joseph was a warlock who would bring a curse on the land. In addition, Joseph followed strange customs that the people of Mazovia could not understand. He refused to eat pork. When he prayed, he wrapped himself in a shawl striped black and white and trimmed with fringes, and turned his face toward the East. At the entrance to his hut he had fastened a piece of parchment that he called a mezuzah. On the Sabbath he neither kindled a fire nor did his goldsmith's work. He also refused to bow before the idols of Mazovia—and he did not like to hunt. Chieftain Wilk soon came to realize that if Joseph

Joseph and Koza

Joseph and Koza

remained among them, there would be a rebellion in Mazovia.

Wilk now tried to persuade his daughter that the stranger was not the right husband for her. But Koza, who had always obeyed her father, suddenly became stubborn. She fell at his feet and said: "I will never love anyone but Joseph. If I cannot be his wife, I will throw myself in the Vistula and the river will have its sacrifice."

"But Joseph cannot remain in Mazovia," Wilk said. "Because of him, the people are divided. If he stays, all will suffer."

"Then I will go with him to Jerusalem," said Koza.

Wilk called his councillors together to seek their advice. Most of them were of the opinion that a young woman's love must be respected. Others argued that it would be an insult to the Chieftain's honour if he gave his daughter in marriage to a stranger who refused to worship the gods of Mazovia. Zla, who did not give up easily, sent a message to the council room announcing that the stars were against the match. However, faith in the stars and Zla's prophecies was no longer strong. The men whose daughters had been sacrificed to the Vistula now accused Zla of being a murderess who had sent to their deaths the most beautiful girls of Mazovia.

When Zla learned that Wilk had agreed to the marriage of Joseph and Koza despite her threats and warnings, she decided to make one final effort to interfere. There were magic powers that could be used only once. If she failed, her power would be destroyed forever. First she fasted three days and three nights, then she lit seven candles made of human fat. When this was done, she shaved off her elf locks and clipped her long, claw-like nails, kneaded these into a lump of dough, and burned it before an image of Baba Yaga, all the while invoking the Evil Powers.

On the fourth night she made her way to a thick forest and, using the most potent incantations and spells, she summoned Baba Yaga and her retinue of devils.

The night was hot and dark. Suddenly a wind arose and a scarlet light appeared. Baba Yaga arrived in her mortar, carrying her pestle in one hand and her tree broom in the other. Her face was like pitch, but her nose was red, turned up, with broad, flaring nostrils. Her eyes burned like live coals. Instead of hair, thistles grew out of her skull, and though she was a woman she had a beard like a man. Her companions rode on brooms, canes, and shovels. Even Topiel, King of the Vistula, came— foaming with rage. The beasts of the forest, frightened by these apparitions, howled and screeched and hid themselves in ditches and tree hollows.

Zla bowed seven times to Baba Yaga. "Mighty Baba! As you already know, a man has come from the faraway city of Jerusalem and his name is Joseph. With cunning words, he has conquered the heart of Chieftain Wilk and won the love of Koza.

Joseph and Koza

Joseph and Koza

Because of him, there was no sacrifice to the Vistula this year. Now he is about to marry Koza. If their marriage takes place, it will mean that we who worship you have lost our right to rule over human fate. I implore you, therefore, not to let this wedding take place."

"There will be no wedding!" Baba Yaga cried in a voice as hoarse as a saw. "I'll sweep it away with my broom and crush it with my pestle."

"There will be no wedding!" Topiel roared. "I will drown it with my waters."

"There will be no wedding!" chorused all the goblins, hobgoblins, sprites, and imps, each in his own shrill voice.

That night Zla went to bed assured that the Evil Spirits would emerge victorious after all. It might have been impossible for them to destroy the crops and bring a flood, but surely they could stop a marriage. But Zla did not know that Joseph possessed the sacred powers of a soothsayer and could see what was happening long distances away.

Joseph and Koza

Joseph and Koza

He knew that Zla had summoned the Evil Forces. He also knew how to overcome them. He prayed to God, and his prayer was heard. On the day of the wedding, Baba Yaga, Topiel, and all the evil creatures were suddenly overcome by a deep sleep. Zla tried desperately to summon them, but they did not wake up.

Since the wedding ceremony could not be performed in the temple of the idols, it took place in the palace garden. Koza's parents and her ladies-in-waiting were the only guests. Joseph placed a golden ring on her first finger and intoned the words of the marriage vow himself. The following day, Joseph and Koza mounted two magnificent stallions, given to them by Wilk, and started on their long journey to the Holy Land. Although the gift of the horses was a very generous one, it did not compare with the crown Joseph had made for Wilk.

It was very difficult for Wilk and Wilkova to part with their only daughter. Koza, too, suffered at leaving her parents. But so it has always been—a wife must go with her husband, especially one who has saved her life. A huge throng accompanied them to the very edge of Mazovia. Trumpets were blown, drums and bells played; at night, torches were lit.

If one left one's country in those days, there was no way to send messages back. One was never heard from again. But somehow the Mazovians learned that Joseph and Koza were living happily in Jerusalem. Joseph's fame as a goldsmith spread far and wide. Koza bore him sons and daughters, who were brought up in the faith that there is only one God.

In Mazovia, from that time on, human sacrifice was forbidden. And later, when Mazovia and the surrounding tribal lands were united into one kingdom, called Poland, the Poles became Christians. Human sacrifice was then abolished throughout the country.

Zla had long since died; and Baba Yaga, Topiel,

Joseph and Koza

and all their evil band were heard about mainly in stories that grandmothers told their grandchildren as they churned butter or wove flax. But for many centuries it was the custom on the first day of summer for the girls of Mazovia to assemble on the shores of the Vistula. They would throw a straw dummy into the river in memory of the maidens sacrificed to Topiel. While the straw girl was bobbing up and down in the current, drifting toward the open sea, they would sing, dance, and celebrate Joseph's rescue of the beautiful Koza.